FIC
PERRY

Perry, Anne.

A dish taken cold.

V. Good

$11.95

DATE	
MAR 7 2001	
MAR 1 8 2001	AUG 7 2001
APR 1 2 2001	SEP 1 8 2001
MAY 2 - 2001	JAN 2 8 2003
	AUG 1 4 2003
MAY 1 7 2001	JAN 2 7 2004
MAY 3 1 2001	JAN 2 5 2005
JUN 2 1 2001	
JUL 1 4 2001	

A DISH TAKEN
COLD

A Dish Taken
COLD

Anne Perry

An Otto Penzler Book

CARROLL & GRAF PUBLISHERS, INC.

NEW YORK

First Carroll & Graf edition 2001

Carroll & Graf Publishers, Inc.
A Division of Avalon Publishing Group
19 West 21st Street
New York, NY 10010-6805

Library of Congress Cataloging-in-Publication Data is
available.
ISBN: 0-7867-0822-0

Manufactured in the United States of America

A Dish Taken
COLD

CELIE STARED AT HER IN TOTAL disbelief. It could not be true. Jean-Pierre dead? How could it be? He had been perfectly all right when she had left him with Amandine only a few hours ago. And there had been no violence in this area last night. Revolutionaries were swarming all over Paris as they had been ever since the storming of the Bastille just over three years ago. The city was in a ferment of ideas, tearing down the old, reforming everything, creating sweeping changes that needed the force of arms to carry them through. The power of the Church was destroyed. The monarchy itself teetered on the edge of an abyss. There was economic chaos, and the hunger and fear that went with it. France was at war, and the Prussian armies were massed on the borders. But for all the imprisonments and executions, no one had yet slaughtered women, let alone babes in arms.

'He can't be!' she said desperately. 'He was . . . he . . . '

Amandine was white-faced with shock herself, and guilt, her eyes hollow. Celie had left the baby in her care because the usual nurse had been called away on some family emergency of her own. Such care was necessary because, since her husband's death over a year ago, Celie had worked for that extraordinary woman of intellect, letters and dazzling conversation, Madame de Staël. She was daughter of Necker, the great minister of finance, and now wife of the Swedish Ambassador, although she was in her late twenties, no older than Celie herself.

Amandine stood in the middle of the kitchen, the smell of cooking around her.

'It is true,' she said quietly. 'He was asleep in his crib when I left him, and when I went back two hours later he . . . he was no longer breathing. He never cried out or made the slightest noise. He was not sick or feverish. I cannot tell you how much I wish I had sat up with him in my arms all night! If I had guessed . . .' She stopped. Words were no use, only an intrusion into an intolerable pain. Celie was filled with it, every part of her mind consumed, drowned by it.

'I want to see him,' she said at last. 'I want . . .'

Amandine nodded and turned to lead the way back to the small room with its window overlooking the courtyard. The crib was in the corner. Celie hesitated, putting off the moment when it could no longer be denied. She went over slowly and stared down at the tiny form, still wrapped in blankets as if he could feel the cold, although it was the hottest August in years. His face was white. He looked asleep, but she knew in her heart he was not. The frail spirit was no longer there.

Still, she picked him up and held him in her arms, rocking him gently back and forth, the tears running down her cheeks.

She had no idea how much later it was when Amandine took him from her and made her drink some hot soup and eat a little bread. There were no formalities to be observed except the civil ones. There were no priests to turn to in Paris. Religion was outlawed; it belonged to the greed, the oppression and superstition of the past. This was the age of reason. But she would have liked the comfort of ritual now, even if it was foolish and meant nothing. There must be a better way to say goodbye to someone you loved, who was a part of your body and your heart, than simply a cold acknowledgement by some citizen official.

SHE RETURNED THE next morning to her work at Madame de Staël's house. Thérèse the seamstress met her at the door.

'Where have you been?' she demanded. 'Madame has been looking for you. My God, you look terrible! Whatever's happened?'

In a shaky voice Celie told her.

'Jean-Pierre?' Thérèse said incredulously. 'He can't be! Oh, my dear Celie, how appalling!' Her fair face was slack with horror, amazement filled her eyes. 'I've never heard anything so awful! Amandine let him die! Why? How? What was she thinking of?'

'Nothing . . .' Celie shook her head. She was finding it difficult to speak. Her voice choked. 'It wasn't her fault. He had no fever, no sickness. He just . . . died. Now, please . . . I . . . I must go and tell Madame why I am late.'

Thérèse stood helplessly.

Celie left and went to the salon to find Madame. It was a gracious room. Only a short time ago the finest minds in France, both men and women, had exchanged wit and philosophy here, talking long into the night, while the Revolution was still a thing of great ideas, of hope and of reason.

Germaine de Staël was not beautiful, but she captivated men and women alike with her charm and her brilliant intelligence. When she saw Celie she drew breath to chastise her, then she saw her face and the words died on her lips.

'What is it? What have you seen, or heard? Sit down. You look about to faint.' She moved a little awkwardly. She was visibly pregnant, although her husband was not presently in Paris.

Celie wanted to get it over quickly. Saying the words again made it more real.

'Jean-Pierre is dead. Last evening. He was with Amandine Latour. I don't know the cause. He just . . . died.'

'Oh, my dear.' Madame put her arm around her and held her tightly. 'How very dreadful. Such things happen sometimes. No one knows why. There can be no grief like it.' She did not offer any more words. She knew there was nothing to say or to do.

Days and nights passed in a grey succession and Celie did not count them. Her tasks were not onerous. For all her proclamations of brotherhood and equality, Madame was heiress to one of the largest fortunes in France, and she still kept an excellent household. It would be a foolish person in these days of hunger and uncertainty who gave up a comfortable position in it.

However, on the evening of 9 August events began which would change that for ever. Celie had gone to bed exhausted, but she could not sleep beyond the first hour or two. She drifted in and out of dreams, memory returning cold and agonizing with each wakefulness. Then at midnight she heard the alarm bells start to ring somewhere over to the north. It was a wretched sound, rapid, hollow and monotonous. Almost immediately it was echoed from another direction, and then another, until it seemed to be everywhere. The darkness was alive with the clangour of fear.

She rose and lit a candle. There was no need for a robe in the heat, but she felt a prickly sense of vulnerability without it, as if she might be caught in her shift without the protection of clothes. There were other sounds in the house now, other people up.

Her throat tightened as she opened the door and

went through the outer room where Thérèse slept. She was not there. She went to the stair. What was happening? The alarm bells were ringing all over the city.

There was another candle at the bottom of the stairs, and in its yellow light she saw the frightened face of one of the menservants.

'What's happening?' she called out. 'What's all the noise?'

'I don't know,' he answered breathlessly. 'It's everywhere.'

Celie went down the stairs and across to the salon. Madame was inside, a dozen or more candles lit and filling the room with yellow light and dense shadow. The curtains were drawn back so she could see out of the windows. Thérèse was at the other door.

'Are we being invaded?' she asked, her voice rising sharply to a shriek.

'No, no!' Madame answered with a shake of her head. She, too, must have felt the need to dress, because she had a plain morning skirt and blouse on. She looked extraordinarily calm, although the hand that held the candelabra was not completely steady. 'Jacques said there is a rumour that the suburbs have risen and are marching on the Palace of the Tuileries.'

'The king!' Celie gasped. 'They are going to murder the king!'

'They may try,' Madame replied grimly. 'They say it is Santerre at the head, and I would put nothing past him. But don't worry, my dear.' She lifted her chin a little higher. 'There are nine hundred Swiss Guard to protect him, two hundred gendarmes and three hundred royalist gentlemen, not to mention about two thousand National Guard. The rioters will quickly be driven back.' She turned to the manservant just as there was a loud noise from the street. 'Still, it would be a good idea to bar the doors and make sure all the bolts are shot. It will all be perfectly all right, a lot of shouting, I dare say, but no more. We should go back to our beds and get what sleep we can.'

But the bells went on all night with their hollow, soulless sound, and then at seven in the morning there was the violent shock of cannon-fire. Celie sat up in bed, the sweat trickling down her body. The air was hot already. Outside there were still people shouting and the tramp of feet. Then the cannon-fire came again, louder and more rapid.

She had kept most of her clothes on and she scrambled out of bed, put on her shoes and ran to the window. There were a dozen men in the street below, bare-armed, many of them wearing the red bandannas and kerchiefs of the rabble who had marched from Marseilles, dregs of the seaport slums and prisons. They were all armed with pikes or sabres. A woman on the far side grabbed at a child and scuttled away into a courtyard, avoiding looking at them. An old man shouted something incomprehensible, a precious half-loaf of bread clutched in his hand.

Celie drew her head in and went downstairs to the salon where Madame and Thérèse were standing in the middle of the floor. Madame was pale but composed. Thérèse's fair gold hair was dishevelled, her blouse was fastened crookedly and she was quite obviously terrified.

'Philippe says the suburbs have risen and are marching on the Tuileries!' she said the moment she saw Celie. 'There are thousands of them and they have cannons! We shall all be killed—'

'Nonsense!' Madame snapped sharply. 'Why on earth should they hurt us? We are daughters of the Revolution, as much for freedom and reform of injustice as they are!' She went over to the window and looked down, but standing back a little so as not to be seen from below. Then she turned. 'I think we should have something to eat, and perhaps some hot coffee.'

It was an order. Celie went to obey and Thérèse followed her. In the kitchen Celie riddled out the old ashes and built a new fire in the stove. It was airless in the room but neither of them wanted to open the door, even into the courtyard.

'How are you feeling?' Thérèse said, her voice dropping with pity. 'I suppose you can hardly care about the king, or anyone else, right now. I wouldn't if I were you.'

Celie watched the flames catch hold, and closed the stove door. There did not seem to be any sensible answer to make. She did not want to talk about Jean-Pierre, although she knew Thérèse meant to be kind. She had no children of her own. She could not be expected to understand. She had had a lover a while back, but apparently it had come to nothing. She had not talked about it.

Thérèse was putting cups onto a tray. They could hear the noise from the street even in here. 'I don't blame you for hating Amandine,' she went on.

'I don't hate her.' Celie denied it, filling the pot with water from the ewer. She was glad she did not have to go out to the well to draw it. 'It wasn't her fault.'

'You're very charitable,' Thérèse said drily.

Celie looked at her, wondering what she meant.

Thérèse shrugged, a little smile curling the corners of her lips. 'Come on, my dear, she did leave him alone! She should have known better. He was so little . . .'

'Stop it!' Celie blurted out. In her mind she saw him lying there, alone, dying. She should not have left him with Amandine. She should have stayed with him herself. Pain filled her till it seemed she could barely hold it.

Thérèse put her arm around her. The gesture did not even touch the coldness inside; it only suffocated, although it was intended as sympathy.

'You are blaming yourself,' Thérèse said softly. 'You mustn't. It is not your fault. No mother stays with her child every minute. You left him with someone you thought you could trust. You must never chastise yourself!'

The water was boiling.

'I can't help it,' Celie admitted. 'I should have been there.' She moved away and fetched the ground coffee. She poured the water and brewed it automatically, smelling the bitter, pungent aroma. There were no clear thoughts in her mind. The noise outside was getting worse.

They returned upstairs and waited in the salon. Some

of Madame's friends arrived and watched with her from the windows. News came every now and again, sometimes shouted from the street, sometimes in the mouth of a breathless servant or visitor.

'The streets are sealed off!'

'All the shops have been closed.'

'The people are evacuated!'

'The Marseillaise are storming the Palace!'

They had known that. They sat huddled together and stared towards the window and the street. Someone else arrived, hot and dirty from running, fighting her way through angry crowds.

'There's a terrible battle going on around the Tuileries!' She dropped her shawl where she stood, a plain brown thing over a drab skirt and blouse. It was the only dress that was safe these days. 'They're killing people everywhere! I saw half a dozen Marseillaise hack a man to death just a hundred yards from here. They've gone mad.'

Thérèse stifled a scream.

Celie felt only a distant horror, but it was something of the mind. Her heart was already numb.

'There are two thousand National Guard at the Palace,' Madame said with confidence. 'Not that they will be needed. The Swiss Guard will turn the rabble.'

Celie and Thérèse went to fetch more coffee. It was not really needed, but it was something to do.

'I wish I were as brave as Madame,' Thérèse said confidentially as they were boiling the water again. She looked at Celie with wide, frightened eyes. 'And I admire you so much. Your courage is superb. And your forgiveness.'

'The Marseillaise have done nothing to me,' Celie replied.

'Not the Marseillaise,' Thérèse said impatiently, waving her hand. 'Amandine . . . and, of course, Georges.'

Celie was confused. 'Who is Georges?'

Something tightened in Thérèse's pretty face and her voice changed tone. 'Her lover, of course. You didn't know that?'

'Why should I be angry with him?' She did not care; it was simply automatic to ask, easier than trying to convince Thérèse that none of it mattered. Jean-Pierre was dead. Nothing else was completely real.

The water was boiling but Thérèse ignored it, staring back.

'Because if Georges hadn't been there, Amandine would have been holding your baby, talking to him, instead of in bed with Georges! Are you really so stunned you had not yet thought of that?'

It had never occurred to her. Jean-Pierre's death had been accidental, one of those terrible tragedies one never understands, something for which there is no reason.

'I'm sorry,' Thérèse said with quick gentleness. 'Perhaps I shouldn't have said anything. It's just that in your place I wouldn't have the forbearance you have, and I wanted you to know that I admire you. I would want revenge! A life for a life. I wouldn't be able to think about anything else.'

Before Celie could reply there was a noise in the courtyard, footsteps, shouting, then Jacques, one of the menservants, hurled himself in through the door, his face streaked with blood.

'The National Guard have turned!' he gasped. 'They've gone over to the Revolutionaries! Half the Swiss Guard is massacred. The king's gentlemen are being slaughtered and their bodies thrown out of the windows. In the streets everyone who even looks like an aristocrat is being put to the sword.'

The pot boiled over and no one noticed.

An hour later they were upstairs, terrified to hear the news that came up from the street about quarter-hourly. Six hundred of the Swiss Guard were dead. All the king's gentlemen. No one knew what had happened to the gendarmes. Probably they were dead too. The Tuileries was on fire. The flames were not visible from here, but the pall of smoke hung in the sky, darkening the sun, closing in the heat.

Noon came and went.

It was true. Santerre was at the head of the mob. He had demanded the king's surrender.

'Never!' Madame said fiercely. She was mortified at the slaughter of her compatriots in the Swiss Guard. 'He has more courage!'

But in that, too, she was mistaken. The queen made as if to resist, but the king, perhaps to save even greater bloodshed, walked out and calmly submitted, offering up himself and his family to be taken into imprisonment at the Temple.

Madame was distraught. She had many personal friends among the Swiss Guard and, in spite of all that anyone could do to dissuade her, she insisted on taking out her carriage, and going to see if she could save or help anyone. She seemed oblivious of the danger to herself.

Celie went to bed exhausted and frightened, but the heat was intense, the air seemed to clog in the throat and there was still shouting and the march of feet outside in the street. She ached with loneliness, and when snatches of sleep came, Jean-Pierre was there in her arms again, alive, smiling up at her. On each awakening the cold hand of grief tightened inside her with the same shock as the first time. It was hard not to hate Amandine and the unknown Georges. Perhaps she had been to blame. Maybe she had lied, and Jean-Pierre had cried out, but she had been too busy making love to hear him, or maybe she had simply ignored him, thinking it would not matter.

That day, 11 August, there was more news which outraged Madame de Staël.

'Take away the liberty of the press!' she said furiously, her face flushed, her eyes blazing. 'That's impossible! It is against everything the Revolution stands for! What liberty have we if we cannot write what we believe?'

It was typical of her that she should think of writing first. She was a passionate and eloquent writer of articles, novels, pamphlets, memoirs, anything and everything. To communicate was the breath of life to her, the purpose of existence. Now the new order had in one stroke betrayed all who believed in it. She stormed back and forth, wringing her hands, then at midday, disregarding her condition, she went out without an explanation or any word as to when she would return.

Thérèse went to see if she could buy bread, cheese, perhaps a few onions, and some more coffee. Celie tidied the salon and had Jacques draw water so she could do a little laundry.

Thérèse came home with bread and onions, but no cheese. Her face was smutted and even her hair had tiny flakes of ash from the still-smouldering ruins of the Tuileries. 'I don't know why you're bothering to wash!' she said angrily. 'It'll be worse than when you started. I can hardly breathe for the smell of smoke, and there are flies everywhere. It's as hot as damnation, and the corpses are beginning to smell already. I wish I were anywhere but Paris. I don't know why we stay here!'

'There's civil war in the Vendée and Brittany,' Celie replied flatly. 'We're at war with Prussia. Where do you want to go?'

'Well, I can understand you staying here,' Thérèse said with a shrug. 'But you'd better do whatever you're going to before Madame decides to leave. You can't remain alone! What will happen to you? You have no one.'

Celie thought of Amandine. She had believed her a friend, but perhaps she was wrong.

'What is this Georges like?' she asked curiously.

Thérèse's lips tightened. 'He's handsome enough, in a brash sort of way.'

'I don't care what he looks like!' Celie said sharply. 'I mean what does he believe? Is he clever or brave? Is he honest?'

'Georges?' Thérèse laughed, a curiously brittle sound in the hot, close air of the kitchen filled with the smell of steam and wet linen. 'I don't know what he believes. Whatever is popular at the moment. The king, Necker, Mirabeau, Lafayette, everybody in their turn. Now I suppose it is the Girondins, and if the mob rules then Marat, or whoever.'

'That's contemptible!' Celie said with disgust. 'Why does Amandine have anything to do with him?'

'Because he's charming and funny, he tells her what she wants to hear, and I suppose he's good in bed!' Thérèse said bitterly. 'Haven't you ever been in love . . . with someone who made you feel happy, and it wasn't difficult to let yourself believe they meant all they said?'

Celie thought of her husband Charles. It had been a pleasant relationship, friendly, reliable. She could not recall him making her laugh, or telling her the things her heart wanted to hear. But he had been honest and, in his own way, brave.

'Georges knows how to make people like him,' Thérèse went on. 'It's a very useful talent, and he knows that.'

Celie turned away. It sounded shallow and manipulative. How could Amandine have given her body, let alone her heart, to someone so worthless? And while she was with Georges, Jean-Pierre had died . . . alone . . . no one holding him, no one helping, no one even knowing. It was a cheap and shabby betrayal of trust, of what she had thought was friendship. Thérèse was right—if Madame left, there would be nothing here in Paris for Celie. She would be alone.

A WEEK WENT by. The weather was suffocating, but slowly the ash cleared, the bodies of the dead were taken away. A new rhythm settled in. The press was censored, but in all the streets one could buy Marat's *L'Ami du Peuple*, filled with cries for vengeance, rivers of blood to wash away the corruption of the old ways. Hebert's *Père Duchesne* made the vulgar laugh with its coarse lampoons of the royal family. Madame de Staël visited her friends, grieved with them in their losses, planned for the future and, as always, talked of ideas.

On the 19th came news that shocked her deeply. The Marquis de Lafayette, hero of the American struggle for independence, early champion for new freedom in France, had defected to the Austrians—the enemy whose armies were even now poised to invade France!

Celie had expected Madame to shout, to explode in words of anger or hurt, disbelief, even the all too understandable desire for revenge. Instead, Madame sat beside her bed in the candlelight looking startlingly tired. She was so young, not yet thirty, but now she had deep circles under her eyes and no colour in her skin. She was visibly heavier around the waist and hips with the child she was carrying. This time last year, in the heat of the summer, Celie had been like that. She could feel it as if it were only a day ago.

'How could he do that, Celie?' Madame asked, staring up, her eyes shadowed. 'How can he betray everything he's stood for—and to the Austrians, of all people?'

'I suppose he was afraid,' Celie replied wearily.

'That's no reason! We're all afraid! God knows, there's enough to be afraid of. I don't know which is worse, the armies on the borders or the mob here.'

'The mob here at least are French,' Celie said, setting down the water jug, forgetting for a moment that Madame was Swiss and her absent husband Swedish.

'A coward?' Madame said bitterly. 'Not Lafayette! Never!'

'Then perhaps he just stopped believing in anything,' Celie suggested.

'That is the ultimate cowardice,' Madame retorted with ringing conviction. 'If you haven't even the courage to hope, to care, to want, to what purpose are you alive at all?' She shook herself impatiently. 'Of course we all despair at times, but only for a moment! You rest, or you mourn, you heal: then you take heart and begin again.' She stood up and came to Celie, putting her arms around her. 'You will heal, my dear. Not quickly, of course—and you will never forget. But you will go on. It has always been women's lot to give life, to love, to have joy and fear, and sometimes to lose. But we do not stop living. That would be a dishonour to life itself, and Jean-Pierre was part of life.'

Celie took a step back, willing herself to be angry rather than weep. She swallowed on her aching throat.

'Doesn't Lafayette's betrayal make you angry?' she demanded. 'Can you bear that Lafayette, of all people, deserted us for the enemy, and not hate him for it?'

'No, I can't,' Madame admitted, going back to the bed and flopping onto it, her fists clenched. 'I want to shout at him, to hit him as hard as I can with my bare hands and feel the sting of flesh. I want him to know how I feel. But, since he's in Austria and I'm here, that's impossible!'

Celie went back through Thérèse's room to her own. She knew Thérèse was still awake, but she said nothing. Amandine was not in Austria—she and Georges were both still here, in noisy, suffocating, blood-drenched Paris. There was one betrayal at least which could be avenged. She did not yet know how, but there would be a way. It was only a matter of finding it.

ON 23 AUGUST the Prussian armies advanced and Longwy fell before them. The news reached Paris with a high, sharp pitch of fear, as if invasion were only days away. Madame was still struggling to assist those of her compatriots she could find, and for whom there was any encouragement or assistance to give.

Celie had not seen Amandine since Jean-Pierre's death. It was a friendship whose loss cut her. She had expected Amandine to visit her more often, not less, after the tragedy. She said nothing about it, but nevertheless she caught a knowing look in Thérèse's eye, and was pleased she had the tact not to put words to it.

The following afternoon they were out walking slowly in the sun, talking of nothing in particular. Incredibly, there were still acrobats performing on the pavements, and a marionette show, as if life were just as always.

'The theatres are still playing,' Thérèse remarked with wonder. 'I don't know how they can.'

'I suppose they have to eat, like anyone,' Celie answered, turning to watch as a group of National Guardsmen came around the corner, red, white and blue cockades in their hats, muskets over their shoulders.

'But everything they put on is so boring,' Thérèse went on. 'It's all the same propaganda now. Half of it doesn't even make sense!'

'Because all the meaning has been censored out of it,' Celie agreed, moving closer to Thérèse as a youth raced past them and ran into the opening of a courtyard. His feet clattered over the cobbles and they heard him banging with his fists on the wooden door beyond.

The guardsmen drew level with them and stopped.

'Is that Citizen Carnot's house?' one of them asked Celie, pointing to where the youth had disappeared.

'I don't know,' Celie replied.

'Don't lie, Citizeness,' he said grimly, fingering his

musket. 'His father-in-law is an enemy of the Revolution. We have a warrant to search his house. Who was it who just went in?'

'Not his father-in-law!' Celie said tartly.

'So you knew him!' The man was triumphant, his suspicion proved. One of the men behind him brought his gun to the ready.

Thérèse grasped hold of Celie's arm tightly, her fingers biting into the flesh.

'No, I don't know him.' Celie kept her voice level, her eyes steady. 'But he was about eighteen. He couldn't be anybody's father-in-law.'

The man looked at her narrowly, then apparently decided he could not exactly name the fault he saw in her and turned away. He waved his arm peremptorily and ordered his men into the courtyard.

'Poor devil,' Celie said quietly.

'You don't know who he is,' Thérèse pointed out. 'He could be anybody. He could be a real enemy of the people. He might be hoarding food, planning to help the royalists, or harbouring a priest or something.'

'The priest could be his brother!'

'Everybody's somebody's brother,' Thérèse said sharply. 'That doesn't make it all right to hide them. Come

on! If we stay here they might think we are involved!'
She tugged at Celie's sleeve.

'Amandine lives only a few doors away from here,'
Celie retorted without moving. She had not been here
since that night. 'I wonder if she knows these people . . . '

'What does it matter?'

There was shouting from inside the house. Someone
was banging a gun butt furiously against the door. A
woman screamed. There was a volley of shots, and then
silence.

Somewhere opposite a child started to cry.

Two old women were quarrelling at the end of the
street, regardless of the whole thing.

The guardsmen appeared again, marching out of the
courtyard, a man, his arms pinned by his sides, between
the first two. He was bruised and bloody. He looked
about thirty, dressed in ordinary, brown working
clothes. Behind him, also held close by guardsmen, was
a second man, older, his hair thin, his face very white
but held high as if he would not give in to the fear
which shook his body. After them a single guardsman
half dragged a woman who was cursing at him, swear-
ing and pleading alternately, her feet tripping as she
fought to keep her balance.

'They must have been hiding him after all,' Thérèse observed with a grimace. 'The boy was too late to warn them. It doesn't do to hide a wanted person. It brings ruin down on your whole family, and it doesn't save them in the end.'

The guardsman let the woman go and gave her a little push. She stumbled and fell, remaining where she was, tears running down her face.

Perhaps it was not a wise thing to do, but Celie went over to her. She considered for a moment trying to help her up, then changed her mind and squatted down beside her.

'Is it your father they've taken?' she asked.

The woman nodded.

'What has he done?'

'Nothing! A few pamphlets, but that was before the press was stopped!'

'Then he'll probably be all right. Have you someone you can go to?'

The woman shook her head.

There was a noise further up the street, doors opening and closing. Celie was aware of someone standing over her.

'Where did they take him, Minette?' It was a man's voice, very deep, almost husky.

'I don't know,' the woman on the pavement replied. 'They didn't say.'

Celie looked up. The man who had spoken was very dark; his hair sprang back from his brow in heavy waves. His eyes were almost black as she looked at him with the sun at his back. There was gentleness in his face, and it seemed as if in other times he would laugh quickly, and perhaps lose his temper just as quickly.

He held out his hand to Minette and, against her will, hauled her to her feet.

'Well, we had better find out,' he said, his jaw tightening. 'You're no use to anyone sitting here. I suppose it was the pamphlets again? It will probably be the Commune. What did he write this time?'

'Nothing!' Minette lied futilely.

The man looked at Celie, a slight smile on his lips. 'Are you all right, Citizeness?'

Celie scrambled up, dusty and rather awkward. 'Yes . . . thank you . . .'

His smile broadened, then he took Minette by the elbow and walked away. He did not seem to have seen Thérèse who stood half in the shadows against the far wall, her face set hard, her mouth thin, eyes narrow and bright.

Celie walked more slowly, without talking again.

Thérèse kept darting sidelong glances at her, but she held her tongue. Celie could not get the 'domiciliary visit,' as they were known, out of her mind. She had seen them before, of course, and heard of them from friends. Everyone in Paris knew that the Revolutionary powers could search your house any time they suspected you of harbouring a wanted person, an enemy of the Commune or of the government. All priests were automatically in that category. Religion was a superstition from the past, an oppressor of the poor. To sustain it, even to the least degree, was to stand in the way of progress, and justice, and the true freedom, that of reason, enlightenment and the brotherhood of equality.

She could not forget Amandine, sneaking off and leaving Jean-Pierre alone so she could be with her lover, the flattering, manipulative Georges. It was the betrayal which hurt. She had liked Amandine as much as anyone. She had trusted her completely—she would never have left Jean-Pierre with her otherwise. Just one hour's selfishness, indifference to a tiny child—and look what it had cost! Celie would pay the price of it for ever.

Another domiciliary visit in that street, that would be the answer. A march down to the Commune between guardsmen, a trial, the fear and the humiliation. Then the sick misery as you thought of the short journey in the tumbrels, the scarlet blade of the guillotine, the plank slippery with blood, the waiting crowd . . . and then oblivion.

Of course they could not execute Amandine. She would be innocent of any wrong as far as they were concerned. What she had really done would not interest them. They would let her go again. And Georges? Well, if he were not really guilty of anything, they would have to let him go too. That was less important. From what Thérèse had said, Amandine would only be hurt by him, sooner or later. Perhaps it would be easier to grieve for him as a martyr than have him live on, and be disillusioned. Then even the past was soiled and stripped away.

She did not yet know how to do it, but that would come.

It took her another two days to call up the nerve to visit Amandine. She found she was shaking as she combed and pinned her hair in front of the piece of glass. The reflection she saw was pale, wide eyes dark with pain and anxiety, mouth turned down a little by sadness, looking vulnerable and lonely. She turned away and walked swiftly downstairs. Madame was out again. She was always out these days. Where she found the strength no one knew.

This was a private matter. She went out into the street and turned left. It was still most unpleasantly hot. The air was sticky. There were little flies everywhere and the smell of the drains was worse than usual. There had been no rain to carry the effluent away. The heat shimmered up from the stones, making them seem to waver.

She walked quickly. Never do anything to attract the guardsmen, or the mob, least of all the Marseillaise with their open shirts and red kerchiefs. Avert your eyes as you pass, in case you seem to be challenging them or, worse, inviting them.

She passed a few people she knew.

She reached Amandine's house and hesitated, gulping and swallowing air. She thought of Jean-Pierre and knocked, then wished she had left it a little longer. But it was too late. The door swung open. Amandine stood there, her eyes blue and smiling, the sunlight on her hair.

'Celie! I'm so glad you've come. I called to see you twice, but you were out or not well.'

'Did you?' Celie said doubtfully.

'Thérèse told me. But it doesn't matter.' She stood aside. 'Come in. Let me get you a little wine and water. It's too hot for coffee. Have you noticed the leaves are beginning to die? And it isn't even September yet.' She led the way into her cool kitchen looking towards the north.

She poured the wine and water and offered Celie a glass. The kitchen was homely, lived in. There was a faint aroma of bread and coffee. Amandine sat down opposite her, her hands cupped around her own glass, as if the coolness of it were welcome.

Then Celie noticed with a jolt a man's coat on a hook on the back of the door to the courtyard, hung casually, as if he knew he would be back. Georges? Was he so comfortable here he took it all for granted?

'How are the people down the street who were arrested?' she blurted out.

'The father-in-law is still in prison,' Amandine replied, looking down at the table. 'They let René go. I think for Marie's sake he pleaded innocence.'

'What do you mean?'

'Said he didn't know his father-in-law was wanted,' Amandine explained. 'It's not true, of course, but what good does it do anyone for him to be executed as well? He feels wretched . . . guilty for being alive, desperately relieved, ashamed. How did you know about it?' Her eyes searched Celie's.

'I was passing at the time,' Celie said truthfully. 'How is Minette?'

'Terrified,' Amandine answered with a twisted smile, looking up at Celie sadly. 'Angry, confused, waiting for them to come back again, trying not to hope her father will be freed because she wants it so much, and trying not to face the fear that they'll guillotine him because she can't bear it. She wanted René to say what he did, but she's furious with him, too, for being alive.' She was watching Celie as she spoke, to see if she understood.

Celie had not lost anyone to the Revolution. Charles had died in an accident. Jean-Pierre's death had been due to carelessness, neglect.

Amandine looked down at her hands again. 'Anyway, how are you? Madame de Staël must be very upset about the censorship. I know she is a great writer.'

Before Celie could reply, the door from the courtyard opened silently and a man came in. He was handsome in an easy, obvious way. Celie recognized him immediately. It was he who had tried to help the woman Minette in the street two days ago. He looked first at Amandine with a quick light of pleasure, almost a softness; then he turned to Celie, and just as she knew him he, too, remembered her. He smiled and it lit his dark face.

Celie felt herself stiffen.

'Hello, Georges,' Amandine said gently. 'You don't know Celie Duleure. She works for Madame de Staël.' She turned to Celie. 'Georges Coigny.'

'Citizen Coigny,' Celie answered with a cool smile. She was disconcerted that he should be the man who had seemed to behave with such gentleness at that incident. She did not wish to share anything with him. She wanted to leave, but she would be spoiling her own purpose if she did. She ought to stay and learn something about him. It was ridiculous to rely on the snatches that Thérèse had told her. She thought of Jean-Pierre alone and dying in this very house, only a few yards from where she was sitting now, and steeled herself.

Georges sat down as if he did not need to be invited, and Amandine accepted it. There was not even a flicker of surprise in her face. She looked equally comfortable, except that there was concern in her soft features as she regarded Celie.

'Will you stay and eat with us?' she asked. 'It is only vegetable stew, but we should enjoy your company.'

'Thank you.' The words sounded hollow, as if she were speaking a foreign language she barely understood. 'It is just what I should like. And this room is lovely and cool.'

Amandine smiled and stood up, ready to busy herself with the meal, like a good hostess. Celie watched her with envy for her quiet, domestic happiness. She glanced across at Georges, and saw his eyes on her as well. She loathed him for his complacency. He was as much responsible for Jean-Pierre's death as Amandine. But for his selfishness, his intruding appetites, Amandine would never have left him.

Georges turned to Celie. 'How are you managing with the food shortages, Citizeness?' he asked. 'I heard the baker on the Rue Mazarine has bread most days. It's a little walk, but it's worth it.'

Celie did not want his helpful advice. She stared at him. There was nothing in his eyes even to suggest Jean-Pierre crossed his thoughts. Was he tactful, not wanting to hurt her, not bring it to her mind unnecessarily? Or was he simply callous? He could not be unaware of it. He must have been there, seen Amandine's horror . . . the guilt.

'Thank you.' She hoped she did not sound as stiff as she felt. He must not suspect. Her slowly unfolding plan depended on them both being unaware. She made herself smile. 'I shall remember that. Rue Mazarine?'

'Yes. I think times may get harder.'

'Do you?' That was something she had not thought of. All her emotions were in the past; the future hardly mattered, except to find some sort of justice.

His face was grave. 'I can't help but think so. They are talking of trying the king, and I think it is bound to happen.'

'Trying the king?' It had not occurred to her. 'Who? The Convention?' It seemed a preposterous idea, but even as she questioned it she recalled hearing one of Madame de Staël's friends speak of it.

'Naturally,' he said, biting his lip. 'It will give an appearance of legality to whatever they do to him afterwards.'

Amandine was busy with pans on the stove, chopping more herbs to add. She shot a warning glance at Georges, but he was not looking at her. His attention was focused on Celie. There was a warmth in him as if he liked her. It was a facile charm, deliberate and false, and she despised it. Manipulation of people's emotions was contemptible.

'You mean to imprison him?' she asked, frowning.

'Or the guillotine,' he said quietly.

'The guillotine! Execute the king?' Suddenly the room seemed not pleasantly cool in the August heat but chilly, a shiver passing over the skin. 'Do you think so?'

'They'll have to.' He leaned forward a little, his dark eyes troubled. He smelled very faintly of clean cotton and the warmth of skin. A wave of loneliness engulfed her for Charles, not for his nature or his words but for the closeness of being cared for. She stared at Georges, blinking back her misery.

He must have seen the wretchedness in her, and mistaken it for awe or fear.

'They have to!' He searched for the right words with which to explain to her. 'As long as the king is alive, there will be plots centred about restoring him. He isn't an evil man, but you know yourself he tends to take whatever counsel was given him last. Each faction thought they had persuaded him to reason, and then someone else spoke to him, and he changed his mind. No one will trust him . . . they can't.'

She knew it was true. She had lived through all the changes of fortune from the first pleas for reform, through the ascendancy of Madame de Staël's father, then of Mirabeau, then the Girondins. Now the real power seemed to be with the Commune of Paris, and the fearful Jean-Paul Marat.

As if picking her thoughts out of the air, he contin-ued. 'Can you really believe Marat and his hordes would let him live?' he asked softly. 'Have you seen Marat, or heard him?'

She had done both. Marat was half Swiss, half Cor-sican, swarthy, pock-marked and now riddled with some scabrous disease which broke out in suppurating lesions and caused him to hop, almost crabwise, in his pain. His hair had been matted with filth, he wore rags and a red bandanna around his head. Sometimes he even went barefoot, as if in total identification with the sunken-eyed, copper-faced crowds of the dispossessed whom he led. Celie had been no closer to him than three or four yards, and yet she had been aware of the stench of his body. His voice had been hoarse when he spoke, as if his throat were permanently sore. But it was his rage which she remembered above all else, his de-mand for rivers of blood to avenge past injustice, the tearing out of tongues, the splitting of limbs, the cutting of endless throats.

'No . . .' she said huskily. 'No . . . I suppose not.'

'And then everything will change,' Georges went on.

Amandine turned from what she was doing, her brow puckered. 'Won't that be good? Then we can have the real reforms! We can have some proper equality, pensions for the old and the sick, for widows, especially of soldiers. They were talking about that in the Convention only the other day. Alphonse told me, at the Café Procope.'

Georges's eyes were tender as he looked back at her.

'Alphonse is naive, and wants to please. God help him, he wants to be happy! But think about it—we will be leaving behind all the known boundaries of our society. We have outlawed the Church and done away with God, or the hope of divine justice. When we have got rid of the king, and the aristocracy as well, what is there left to fear, or to respect, or even to be certain of—'

'Stop it!' Amandine said sharply, her face tight and pale. 'If you speak like that, people will think you are against the Revolution! Celie's all right, but you don't know who else is! Be careful, Georges!' There was urgency in her voice, and a rising note of fear, not for herself but for him.

Celie waited, her heart pounding. She could not help staring at Georges. His words whirled in her head. What he said was true. They would be entering a new and totally unknown age, everything familiar hurled away. It was frightening.

'All the old restraints would be gone,' Amandine

went on firmly, looking at Georges, then at Celie and back again. 'The rules that crippled us and held us back, the bonds that kept us to our place.'

'The chains of slavery,' Georges mimicked Marat, sounding hoarse and gravelly as he did it. 'And the rules that protected the weak, the old, the foolish and the uncertain will be gone too. Now tell me that we can't have change without blood, and some lives being lost!'

Amandine touched him gently, with no more than a brush of the fingers over his hair. He may barely have felt it, but there was familiarity in it and the certainty of acceptance.

'You know very well I wouldn't tell you anything of the kind,' she answered. 'You can't justify anything with someone else's life. Now, are you going to stop frightening us so we can enjoy our supper? Celie has enough of politics at Madame de Staël's house. You never talked this way with Thérèse.'

His face tightened and he looked away, then turned to Celie.

'I'm sorry, Citizeness,' he said quickly. 'Perhaps I let my tongue run away with me. I thought . . .' He stopped. She knew what he had been trying to say, that she felt the same. She had, and it angered her because for almost an hour she had been snared by his mind, his charm. She had forgotten who he was, and why she hated him.

'There is no need to apologize,' she said very quietly. 'The press is not free, but you can speak your mind in the company of friends. Perhaps you are right, and the changes will not be freedom but chaos instead.'

'He didn't mean that!' Amandine interrupted, her face flushed. She moved a little closer to Georges, and as if unaware she did so, put out her hand. 'Only that we must be cautious not to abuse it. We shall have to take great care . . .'

'I understand,' Celie lied. 'They will be dangerous times—for all of us.' She made herself smile again.

Amandine relaxed. 'Of course. I shouldn't be so . . . nervous. I'm sure you must be hungry. Please, be comfortable. Georges, pass this over, and make room at the table.'

OVER THE NEXT days Celie's mind was in a fever. Georges's face haunted her dreams. Sometimes even awake she could bring him to memory so sharply it was as if he had been in the room with her. And Amandine, whom she had truly believed her friend, had put a few moments' cheap pleasure ahead of Jean-Pierre's life.

Her soft eyes, her frank smile, seemed to rest on Celie's closed eyelids so she could never escape.

But now she needed only a little more knowledge and she would know how to execute justice. Georges's words came back. He had seemed to doubt the very fabric of the Revolution. The more she thought about it, the more she realized he had even questioned the fundamental goodness of change itself! He had said that executing the king could destroy what was precious, as well as what was evil, oppressive and unjust. He had predicted things which to some people could be viewed as disastrous.

Maybe she did not yet know of anything active that he was doing against the Revolution, but it could surely be only a matter of time before he did something.

He had spoken disrespectfully of Marat, even disparagingly. He would not only deserve arrest for his corruption of Amandine and his part in Jean-Pierre's death, but for quite genuine political reasons. No stretching of the truth would be necessary for Celie, as a good citizen, to warn the officials of the Commune that he was an enemy of the people and, if left free, might do serious harm to the cause of the reforms which, heaven knew, were generations overdue.

But to be effective, to catch Amandine as well, Georges must be arrested in her house. Celie needed to know more of his actions, his habits, his comings and goings.

It was not difficult to find an excuse to call again: a few buttons borrowed for Madame's blouse when she could not purchase them; a pair of boots Madame no longer wanted, which fitted Amandine; she was passing on the way home with a few extra onions; a word of thanks about the baker Georges had recommended.

Amandine seemed to suspect nothing. Had she no conscience at all? She still did not mention Jean-Pierre, as if he had not existed. His brief life meant nothing at all. Celie's hope, her joy and her grief did not cross the horizon of Amandine's own happiness with Georges. He was there twice when Celie called, and he behaved with the same manipulative charm, the dark eyes looking at her so directly, the deep velvet voice, the white smile. Her loathing of him increased, for the gulf between what he was and what he pretended to be.

But she learned his comings and goings. He was arrogant enough, sure enough of his charm, and her feminine weakness to it, to be quite unguarded with her. He did not hide his views; he did not even moderate them, except when Amandine warned him. But even she was too sure of herself, and of Celie, to conceal his movements, and the nights he spent in her house . . .

assuredly also in her bed. They must have so little regard for Celie, underneath their pretended warmth, that
for them she was not even a part of their real lives, the
threads of it that mattered. She was not important
enough to be any danger.

But she was! She was very real, and capable of pas-
sion and hunger and pain, intolerable pain. There was
an aching loneliness in her, a grief for a lost baby which
filled the world!

She had all the information she needed. She went to
the Commune, up the stone steps, the heat reflecting
back in a blistering wave carrying the smells of sweat
and dirt. She passed a group of men lounging against
the railings. Many had open shirts and wore red
scarves, or bandannas. Most were unshaven. One was
asleep in the shade, a fly crawling up his arm.

Inside there were self-important citizens going about
their business, footsteps light and quick, eyes sharp, the
intoxicating taste of power on their lips.

She found the right person quickly, almost as if he
had been waiting for her, and fortune guided her footsteps. She told him what he needed to know: Georges's
doubts of the Revolution; his reluctance to try the king
before the people; his dark fears for the rightness of the
cause. Then she told him where she knew he could be

found, on 2 September, for certain. He was a greasy little man, earnest and fussy. He praised her loyalty and her honour, and wrote down everything she said.

She left, telling herself she had served justice and the greater good. She had avenged the loneliness and the pain of Jean-Pierre, who had been too small and too frail to do it for himself. But there was no lightness inside her as she returned home. Her sense of achievement was a hard, tight knot inside her.

Of course, the authorities might not even bother with Georges Coigny. There were dozens of people wanted, maybe hundreds—even one of Madame's own lovers, Louis de Narbonne. In days past she had exerted her influence, and intrigued endlessly to have him made Minister of War. Celie had heard from someone else that Marie Antoinette had laughed aloud, and made a sarcastic remark that now Germaine de Staël would be happy to have all the armies of France at her command! The days when the Queen could joke about anything were long gone. It seemed like another world. And Louis de Narbonne was hunted, as Georges Coigny would be, and probably for as little reason.

She had not meant to think that! The words had slipped out without intent. They were both counter-Revolutionaries, men who would retain the old order with its privilege and oppression and, above all, its in-justice.

Then that very evening she learned accidentally that Madame was hiding de Narbonne here in the house. She should not have been surprised. He had been her lover, which meant he was intelligent, charming, artic-ulate, well read and unquestionably had a vivid sense of humour. Nevertheless, when she came into Ma-dame's bedroom a little after eight, to return some mended clothes, and found Louis de Narbonne, dressed in plain brown breeches and a stained shirt, she felt a chill of fear stab through her and settle like ice in her stomach.

He swivelled around as he heard her footsteps, his hand poised as if to reach for a weapon. He was a handsome man, in a calm, measured way; all intellect and wit, nothing like the obviousness of Georges Coigny.

She smiled at him, as if to see him there was nothing remarkable. Then, when it was too late, she thought she should have said something. He had never worn a countryman's clothes before. He had been elegant, im-maculate. This was an attempt at invisibility. A disguise would have been an admission he was hiding.

She laid the clothes down on the chest at the end of

the bed, then turned and left. Neither of them had spoken.

Downstairs Thérèse was about her business in the kitchen. Jacques was moving bottles of wine, Eduard was busy outside in the courtyard. There was no one else around. The housemaid had gone home, and the grooms and coachmen were above the stables.

'There are more of these awful men from Marseilles in the streets,' Thérèse said angrily. 'Between them and the National Guard, you can hardly walk a dozen yards without being accosted.' If she knew Narbonne was in the house, there was not the slightest sign of it in her manner. She clattered pots about, expressing her irritation with frequent words of exasperation.

Jacques returned and set down bread for the next day, but his face was pale.

'What is it?' Celie demanded.

'I saw a poster on the corner of the street,' he replied, his voice sharp and unhappy. 'Louis de Narbonne is wanted by the Revolution!' He knew Narbonne had been one of Madame de Staël's lovers. All Paris knew it.

Outside in the street someone shouted and there was a roar of laughter. It was all exactly as if there were no one new in the house, certainly no one hunted by the Revolutionary police.

A little before midnight, when Celie was almost asleep, there was a violent banging at the door, as if with a gun butt. She sat up in bed, the sweat breaking out on her body in the hot, suffocating night. Fear knotted inside her. There was a moment's prickly silence, then the banging again.

Celie scrambled out of bed, fishing for a shawl, and went to the door. Thérèse was sitting up, her candle lit.

'What is it?' she demanded. 'What's happening?'

Celie walked past her. 'I don't know.' The banging was still going on. 'I'm going to see if Madame is all right.'

'Why shouldn't she be?' Thérèse said irritably. 'We've got nothing to hide.'

Celie made no reply, but went to the farther door and opened it, peering out. She saw the flicker of a candle as Madame de Staël went downstairs.

Celie hurried after her and Jacques came through from the back of the house, fastening his breeches with clumsy fingers. At any other time he would have been the one to answer the door.

Madame opened the latch just as the National Guardsman raised his musket to bang again.

'Good evening, Officer,' she said courteously, looking at the leader. 'How can we help you?' Her hair was loose down her back, and untidy, and she was dressed for bed, but she spoke as if she had been receiving guests and he was one of them, simply a trifle unexpected.

He was tired and angry, and had felt certain of his errand. Now his expression changed to one of surprise and suspicion. He was perhaps thirty, tall, brown-haired. He might have been pleasant enough to look at had he not been unshaven and exhausted.

'Citizeness de Staël?' he said aggressively.

'Of course.' She smiled at him.

'I've a warrant to search your house.' He made no effort to show it to her. No one argued with the National Guard. That was an offence in itself, and they both knew that.

Her voice did not shake in the slightest nor did her smile waver, but, standing behind her, Celie could see her hands clench and the nails dig deep into the flesh.

'Then you must come in,' Madame said, stepping aside to allow him past. She swallowed and took a deep breath, her shoulders rising and staying high, knotted with tension. 'Who are you looking for?'

'Louis de Narbonne,' he answered immediately. 'He's wanted for treason against France.'

'Oh dear!' She made an effort to keep her voice steady. 'How people change. He used to be an excellent servant of the people, patriotic and loyal. I haven't seen him lately.'

'No?' The man's eyebrows rose sarcastically. 'We know your relationship with him, Citizeness!'

She smiled and looked down. 'I'm sure you do,' she conceded, 'but we are sophisticated people. We understand these things. I'm sure you have been . . . admired . . .'

We! Celie thought in disbelief. She was speaking to this ruffian as if she thought of him as an equal. Everything in him shrieked that he was a peasant, not even a petit bourgeois.

The man stared at Madame de Staël.

'Can I offer you a little wine and water?' she said graciously, still looking only at him, not the half-dozen men behind him. 'It is arduous work you are doing for us. No doubt you have been on your feet all day.'

'Yes, I have,' he conceded.

'Jacques, wine and water for the gentleman,' Madame ordered, barely turning her head as he signalled his men to wait outside. 'Where are you from, Citizen?' she continued. 'I detect a touch of the south in your voice.'

'Provence,' he replied, following her in and closing the door. He seemed pleased she had noticed.

Her face softened and she moved to sit down in one of the large, comfortable chairs. He sat opposite her, glad to rest himself.

'What a beautiful region,' she continued. 'You must find Paris hard, especially this summer with the terrible heat. I've never known it so stifling. And dirty, too, of course, in comparison. Still, Paris is the heart of things, is it not? Surely here we are creating a new order of justice and equality, greater than that in England or Spain or Austria—greater even than the Americas because we have so much more wisdom and greater experience of the past.' Her eyes did not leave his for a moment. 'And then, too, we have a culture and a civilization second to none. Look at our writers! Our scientists, our artists, our poets and painters, and, of course, above all our philosophers. I think philosophy is a French art, don't you?'

'Yes . . .' he answered, struggling to keep up but refusing to admit ignorance of anything. Here was Germaine de Staël, daughter of Necker himself, writer, novelist and supreme conversationalist, addressing him as if he were her equal, as if in another time he might have been invited to her famous salon. 'Certainly,' he answered with gathering conviction. 'We are the most civilized of people. It is in our nature.'

'Don't worry.' She leaned forward confidentially. 'The rest of the world will understand that one day. History will vindicate us totally, Citizen. History will one day say what you and I know now.'

'Of course it will!' he agreed with more feeling. His body relaxed a little. 'We shall be known as heroes then!'

'Your grandchildren will envy you for the time in which you lived,' she said warmly. 'The sights you saw which they will only read about.' She allowed herself to smile at him. 'We are a part of history, Citizen.'

He straightened his shoulders a little.

Jacques returned with the wine and water and hesitated. Celie took it from him quickly and offered it first to the guardsman, who accepted it with relish, then to Madame herself.

The conversation continued. The guardsman ignored Celie and Jacques. Neither dared leave the room. Celie did not even know if Jacques was aware of Louis de Narbonne upstairs in Madame's bedroom. She could think of nothing else. She was cold inside with terror.

She was sweating and her hands were sticky and numb. Surely the guardsman must smell the fear in the room? Or perhaps he was so used to it he no longer recognized it. What did the men outside think he was doing? Searching?

Madame continued to talk. She was interesting, sophisticated, amusing. Now and then the guardsman was reduced to laughter. She spoke of the theatre, of recent inventions, of political and moral philosophy, of art. Celie had never heard her more dazzling. Only the pitch of her voice betrayed to one who knew her so well the fear that tightened her throat and held painfully rigid the muscles of her neck and shoulders.

The guardsman was entranced. Never before had anyone spoken to him as if he, too, were clever, articulate and entertaining. It was the ultimate compliment, the one courtesy no aristocrat had ever afforded him. In his mind he despised her, but it was a hatred born of envy. Tonight she had treated him as if there were no need for it, no cause. For a brief hour he also was of the élite.

He left without searching the house more than perfunctorily.

As the door finally closed behind him Celie found she was shaking uncontrollably. She was gulping as if she could not find enough air to fill her lungs, and her knees had no strength at all. Only now she realized her bodice was soaked with sweat, the ice-cold, clinging sweat of terror.

She looked at Madame de Staël, and saw the recognition in her eyes of exactly the same drenching emotions. For an instant they, too, were equals, their common humanity binding them as one and outweighing everything else.

After a measureless moment Celie turned to Thérèse and saw in her blue eyes only contempt because Madame de Staël had treated Revolutionary ruffians as if they were gentlemen. She did not know about Louis de Narbonne upstairs.

Celie felt colder still, her clothes sticking to her.

'Lock up and blow out the candles,' Madame requested in a voice that trembled. 'We had best all return to our beds.'

Thérèse started to say something, then changed her mind and obeyed.

Celie went up with Madame, a step behind her on the stairs. At the top she turned and smiled. Celie smiled back, hesitantly, her eyes in the candlelight frightened and questioning.

Celie admired her more than anyone else she could

think of, her courage, her willingness to face the enemy and fight with her heart and her wits to save a man she had once loved, even at the risk of her own life. Celie had watched her. She knew the consuming fear, the knowledge of what the cost would be, and yet there had been no hesitation, no weakness or thought of her own safety. It was what she herself wanted to be. She hungered to have that same courage and honour. It was a blazing light in the darkness of corruption, violence and betrayal, disillusion and futility which was engulfing Paris.

But she was not. Sick shame twisted inside her. She had saved no one . . . far from it! The only decisive act she had taken was to betray a man and a woman because they loved each other, and with an hour's indulgence of that love had left a baby alone. Perhaps that made Celie's betrayal justified. It could never make it beautiful.

And she ached for beauty, honour, pity in the tide of hate which rose around her, drowning everything in its ugliness.

She went to her bed with turmoil raging inside her. She had made of herself something she looked at now with loathing. Tomorrow she must find Georges Coigny and warn him, whatever the danger. To fail would destroy her own inner core, the heart and soul of what she was.

BUT THE FOLLOWING morning she had no opportunity to do more than think of Georges Coigny with a dull ache of anguish. Madame had been granted a passport to leave for Switzerland, but she was deeply worried about some of the deputies of the Convention whom she knew were imprisoned in the Abbaye and in grave danger of facing the guillotine.

Citizen Louis Pierre Manuel, the Procurator of Paris, was a well-read man and an admirer of literature. Indeed, he had written the preface to an edition of Mirabeau's letters which he had recently had published. Execrable, in Madame's opinion, but nevertheless at least an attempt at the art of writing. He was approachable. She had written to him requesting an appointment and it had been granted for the democratic hour of seven o'clock this morning.

'You can come with me, Celie,' she said as she walked from her dressing room towards the salon. 'It would be more appropriate if I did not go alone.'

'But . . .' Celie began, but Madame had already passed her and was through the salon door, her back straight, walking very upright. She would not even hear an argument, let alone heed one.

They set out together through the early morning streets. The gutters were worse every day. The smell of coffee-vendors on the corner was pleasant, but they had no time to stop. Every now and then they passed groups of men carrying either muskets or pikes. Some were lounging against walls or the parapets of bridges, others moved idly from one place to another, apparently without purpose, looking for something to occupy their time and feed their anger.

Celie and Madame de Staël walked briskly, eyes forward. There were a few yells and cat-calls, but they were not seriously troubled. At the town hall Madame marched straight up the steps. A National Guardsman at the door moved forward to bar her way, his face sharp, unshaven, suspicious.

'I have an appointment to see Citizen Manuel,' Madame said with great dignity. 'There is a small service I may be able to render him—'

'Indeed?' the man replied with open disbelief. 'And just what service could you render to the Procurator of Paris?'

'That is a private matter of his own, Citizen,' she answered unflinchingly. 'Please tell him Madame de

Staël is here, and that I have considerable admiration for his literary works.' That was a brazen lie, and she told it without a flicker.

Celie was longing for the task to be completed so she could begin the search for Georges. She had named 2 September. She had only twenty-four hours, and now to save him was the thing she wanted most in the world. But Madame had only one thing uppermost in her mind as well, and she was unaware of Celie, except as she needed her for her own support.

They were shown to Manuel's offices and found him more than willing to spare time for a famous lady of letters. Like many other, greater revolutionaries, he had burning aspirations to leave behind him some immortal writings.

Unconsciously he used the manners of the past, his face eager as he recognized her. Celie was invisible.

'Citizeness! In what way can I be of service to you?'

She equivocated only briefly. 'Sir, I appeal to you as a civilized man, which I know you are from your excellent foreword to Mirabeau's letters. And I cannot but believe you are a wise man also . . .'

He flushed with pleasure, although he tried to conceal it.

She did not wait for a reply. She affected not to notice, as if he must be used to such candid praise and it were no more than his due.

'Monsieur, I came to plead for you to exercise the power you have to save the lives of some, at least, of the deputies who now lie imprisoned in the Abbaye, particularly for de Lally and de Jaucourt. They are held for trial and certain death. They are not evil men bent on the betrayal of the ideals both you and I hold so dear. They are simply caught in a misfortune of timing when fear among the masses has caused indiscriminate assets. You and I both know that.' She smiled briefly, not in any lightness of mood but as a mark of her friendship towards him.

Manuel nodded, watching her carefully, his face a trifle pale, his shoulders tight under his brown coat.

'These are times of violent change, often without warning,' she continued. 'Today's heroes are tomorrow's villains. You and I cannot say that next week we shall not find ourselves before a hasty judgment, and taking our last ride in the tumbrels to the Place de la Révolution. In six months you may perhaps no longer have any power. Exercise clemency, Monsieur, so that at least in history you may be found a place among those judged to be above the petty shifts of envy and fear, a man worthy of honour for his ideals and his humanity, as well as his art with words. Reserve for yourself a sweet and consoling memory for the time when it will perhaps be your turn to be outlawed.'

He looked at her, his eyes wide, barely blinking.

Celie wanted to scream, Hurry! Make your decision! There are not only deputies to save, there is Georges Coigny. Innocence and guilt don't matter any more— stop making tiny pointless judgments of an act here or there, preserve a life . . . let me undo what I have done.

Words burst out of her. 'Citizen Manuel . . . in the future we may all be remembered as a violent and bloody people, but what rested in your own heart is what matters. You can do little to help what France does, but what you yourself do lies wholly within your hands.'

Madame looked at her with surprise, but she did not interrupt.

'I long above all things to have a small part in the beauty of compassion,' Celie went on urgently, her voice shaking.

'Of courage, of . . . of . . .' she fought for simple words for the hunger aching within her ' . . . of the love for humanity, not the hatred. I want something good of myself to cling to when my own black hour comes!'

Manuel lowered his eyes. 'Of course,' he said very

quietly. 'Of course, Citizenesses. I shall do what I can, and I believe it may be enough . . .'

Madame de Staël inclined her head in a gesture of gratitude reminiscent of the days of the old regime, and Manuel's face lit with pleasure and at last his body relaxed.

They took their leave, and as soon as they were out of the door, even before they had reached the steps outside or passed the guards, Celie spoke.

'Madame, I, too, have someone I must warn before he is arrested.' It was not necessary to add that arrest in itself almost certainly meant execution. 'Please let me go and search for him!'

Madame's face lit with surprise and pleasure. 'You have found someone to love! I'm so glad, my dear. One should not remain forever a widow, especially someone as young as you are. And Charles was not a great love for you, I know that. You have mourned enough. Do go and warn this man.'

Celie did not bother to explain that Georges was anything but her lover—he was as much as anyone responsible for Jean-Pierre's death, the greatest pain she had ever known. But seeing him executed by the Revolution, and seeing Amandine imprisoned or executed also, would not restore her baby; it would only make of her something ugly she did not want to be. It would rob her of the only beauty left. She simply thanked her and went, breaking into a run as soon as she was in the street.

But where should she go? She knew where Georges would be tomorrow, but not today. The only place to begin was with Amandine, and she dreaded that. She might have to explain!

She would lose Amandine's friendship for ever. There was still a strong yearning of memory and sweetness of hours shared, small kindnesses from her, and it would hurt. Amandine had been careless, selfish, but not with malice. Celie was only too aware of times when she had done the same, grasped at love without thinking of the price. Georges was shallow, manipulative, but he was full of charm and intelligence, and perhaps courage of a sort.

First she tried the places she knew he frequented from her earlier search for enough knowledge to betray him, but he had not been to any of them. Precious time was passing. The sun was high. She was tired. Despair rose inside her. It was mid-afternoon already, and she had accomplished nothing!

With pounding heart and clenched fists she made her way through gathering crowds towards the Rue Ma-

zarine. There seemed to be people everywhere, all talking, shouting, their voices sharp with urgency. She did
not bother to listen to what they were saying. She must
get to Amandine, and ask her where she could find
Georges. She could say she had heard he was wanted.
He did not need to have been betrayed . . . terror and
accusation were in the air. Marat and his hordes from
the tanneries and slaughterhouses of the Faubourg St
Antoine were baying for blood.

She was breathless when she reached Amandine's
door. Please, heaven, she was in! She beat on it, bruising
her fists.

It flew open and Amandine stood there, white-faced.

Celie choked on her own breath. It seemed as if her
heart stopped. She was too late!

'Georges?' she gasped, and choked in a fit of cough-
ing.

'I don't know!' Amandine answered, grasping Celie as
if to rescue her physically from her distress. 'Do you need
him?' Her face held nothing but innocence and fear.

Celie felt an agony of guilt. 'The Commune is after
him,' she said hoarsely. 'I must warn him. Where can I
find him?'

'I don't know.' The colour fled from Amandine's

face, as if she might faint any moment. 'He might be at Citizen Beauricourt's, in the Rue Dauphine.'

Celie broke loose. 'I'll try there. Where else?'

'The Commune itself.' Amandine's voice was no more than a whisper. She held Celie's arm with hard, strong fingers. 'But you can't go there! You could be killed yourself.'

'No, I won't . . .'

'Haven't you heard?' Amandine demanded. 'Verdun has fallen! The Marseillaise are on the march! They are everywhere, attacking, looting, even killing! If Madame can take you, you must get out of Paris!'

'I can't get out of Paris!' Celie shouted back at her. 'I must find Georges and warn him, don't you understand? They're after him! If he comes here tonight, and I heard you say he would, then you'll both be arrested . . . and arrest means death.'

Amandine gulped. 'I know, but there is no use in you dying as well. When he comes I'll warn him—'

'For God's sake!' Celie cried desperately. 'When he comes they could be waiting for him! There'll be no time! I'm going to the Rue Dauphine, and if he's not there to the Commune.'

'I'll come with you.' Amandine stepped forward as if

she would leave without even closing the door behind her.

'No! If you do, there'll be no one here to warn him if I don't find him.'

Amandine hesitated.

Celie threw her arms around her, then let go and turned and ran. She bumped into people, heedless of their annoyance, and plunged on. There were crowds in the streets, milling, jostling, shouting at each other, demanding to know the latest news. She encountered a mob of women on the corner of the Boulevard St Germain, screaming at everyone they saw, faces contorted with rage, hair bedraggled and eyes blazing. Some of them even carried weapons such as kitchen knives and broom handles.

Celie had no time to find another route to the Rue Dauphine. Swallowing her revulsion and a prickle of shame, she hailed them as sisters, and ran on, unmolested, while they surged around a carriage, brought it to a halt and tore open the doors. Celie had no idea what happened to the occupants. She ran on, legs aching, lungs bursting, drenched in sweat.

She came to the house in the Rue Dauphine.

'Georges Coigny!' she gasped to the man who opened

the door. 'Is he here? I must speak with him, it is desperately urgent! Please!'

'No, Citizeness,' he replied. 'I don't know where he is.'

She stared at him, refusing to believe his words. His face was bland, suspicious.

'I want to warn him!' she tried again. 'It is for his good! Please, Citizen?'

'He is not here,' he said. 'Try the Commune. He is sometimes there although, with the Prussians attacking, who knows?'

'Thank you.' Every part of her body ached. She had blisters on her feet and her legs were shaking. But she must find Georges. She could not give up now. If she were ever to regard herself with less than loathing, he must be saved. She started off again along the burning pavements, pushing, elbowing her way towards the huge building where the Paris Commune met.

It was six in the evening and she was close to weeping with fear and exhaustion when at last she saw the dark head of Georges Coigny and found the tears of relief running down her face.

'Georges!' She had meant to shout, but her voice could only croak. 'Georges!'

He heard her over the din and turned. 'Celie!' His brows drew down and his face creased with anxiety. He forced his way over to her, pushing past a man with a huge belly and another stained with the grime of the tanneries. 'What are you doing here? Go home!' He was beside her now. 'Better still, get out of Paris. Haven't you heard the news? The men who marched up from Marseilles are looting and killing in the streets.'

'I know!' she gasped, 'but I need to tell you. You are wanted . . . there is a warrant out for you. You must get out of the city . . . please! They'll guillotine you if they catch you. Go!'

'You must go too,' he urged, putting his arm out as if physically to guide her away. He glanced around, then pushed her along, gently, as if they were old friends. She found herself on the stairs, jostled by people coming and going. The noise was becoming louder, harsher. Someone roared with laughter.

They were out on the street now, Georges's arm still around her, holding her closely. She could feel his body as she was one moment knocked against him, the next almost torn away. A huge man with a barrel chest lurched into her. He stank of stale sweat, onions and rough wine. Involuntarily she cried out, stumbling and only regaining her balance because Georges had not let go of her.

They made their way slowly along the street towards the river. Behind them the shouting grew worse. Someone began to sing, a loud, jubilant sound, like a call to war. Others took it up.

'You must leave Paris!' she shouted at Georges. 'Take Amandine! Get away, be safe . . .' It was the last thing she said to him. A group of men came massing along the street, filling it from side to side, and she was torn from Georges's grip and carried along by them, her cries drowned in their bawdy laughter, and then that song she would come to hate above all others, which would chill the blood in her veins, the 'Marseillaise.'

She could not find Georges again. She looked desperately, knowing it was hopeless. That crowd could have carried him along in any direction. Exhausted and filthy, bruised, her skirts torn, she returned home. She had done all she could. At least Georges knew, and he would protect Amandine.

The following day, 2 September, Madame de Staël determined to leave Paris. Everything she meant to take with her, which was little enough, was piled into a fine coach with six horses, footmen and coachmen in livery, and she and Celie set out.

It was a disastrous plan. They were hardly beyond the entrance to the mews when, at the sound of the postilion's whips, a band of women, gaunt-faced, eyes filled with hatred, hurled themselves at the horses, screaming abuse. The animals were terrified. One reared up, knocking against the others.

'Thieves!' an old woman shrieked, glaring through the windows at Madame and Celie. 'Robbers! Oppressors of the poor!'

'Blood-sucking parasites!' another swore vociferously.

'Plunderer! Looter!' The cries and howls went on. ' "Thief of the nation's gold". '

More people joined in, men as well, until there was a large crowd.

'Take her to the section!' a man yelled, his face twisted with fury. 'Make her answer to the Assembly!' He seized the lead horse's head, while another pulled the postilion from his position, punching him while he did so.

The carriage lurched forward again. Madame was white-faced, but after a glance at Celie she sat back, knowing it would be futile to argue.

At the section offices, they were questioned and abused, charged with trying to smuggle outlaws into

exile. Celie thought of Georges with a hope too fragile
to dare to dwell on and a fear which filled her with
pain. She could not even say Amandine's name to herself. Somehow it had become as important to her to
save them as if she were doing it for Jean-Pierre. This
was her last gift to him, a gift of saving not destroying,
of love above hate. There was hate everywhere, rivers
of it, seas of it. It was drowning them all.

The section officer ordered that they should be taken
under escort across Paris to the town hall. A gendarme
even rode inside on the passenger seat opposite them.
At first he was gruff to the point of rudeness, then, as
Madame's condition became apparent to him, he
treated her with more courtesy. At last, when they were
screamed at, abused, buffeted so violently it was a mar-
vel the horses were not injured, he promised to defend
them, even should it be at the cost of his own life.

Others were very different, perhaps even touched
with guilt at their behaviour towards a woman so obviously with child. Then, the angrier for it, they hurled
abuse, even stones, at the proud carriage with its mag-
nificent horses.

At the town hall they alighted amid an armed mul-
titude, all brandishing clubs, staves, pikes and swords.
They were forced to walk under a vault of spears. One

man with an unshaven face lowered his weapon and pointed it at Madame. Had it not been for the gendarme defending her with drawn sword, she would have fallen, and Celie had no doubt the mob would have been on them both like a pack of dogs.

Inside it was safer, but they were harried and pushed from one official to another, questioned, accused, insulted, until finally, as if God-sent, Procurator Manuel appeared and conducted them to his office. He looked grey-faced, his eyes filled with horror and despair.

He closed the door once they were inside, leaning against the handle as if it supported his weight.

'Thank God I was able to rescue your friends yesterday,' he said huskily to Madame. 'Today I think it would be too late! The Marseillaise are everywhere. Marat's hordes from the slums and tanneries are on the march, howling for blood, and no one seems able to stop them. I don't know if anyone is even trying! Marat calls for seas of blood to cleanse us from the past. Robespierre seems to be going along with him. You must get out of Paris, Madame. I will keep you here safely if I can, then tonight, under cover of darkness, I will get you to the Swedish Embassy. From there you will be able to escape.'

'Thank you, Monsieur,' she said gravely, her voice

quivering a little. She sat down on the chair he provided. He offered one to Celie also, and she was glad to sink onto it. Every part of her hurt, the muscles of her neck, her back tight with fear, her stomach knotted, the pulse pounding in her ears, her skin prickling with fear. The room was insufferably hot, and yet she was cold inside.

Manuel left. Hour after hour they sat there, hearing the screams and howls of the mob muted beyond the closed door. Now and again there were footsteps outside. They hardly dared to breathe, looking at each other in a desperate new companionship forged in the face of death.

Then the footsteps passed and they relaxed for a few moments, until the next time.

For six terrible hours they were there, then at last Manuel returned and they made their way in his own carriage under cover of loud and sultry darkness to the Swedish Embassy.

It was one of the worst nights in the history of France. The Marseillaise stormed the prisons and murdered over thirteen hundred of the inmates, sometimes hacking them limb from limb. Many were old men, women and children, incarcerated for no greater reason than poverty. The Princesse de Lamballe, sometime friend of Marie Antoinette, was torn apart and her entrails cooked and eaten. The gutters of Paris ran with human blood.

In the morning Celie and Madame de Staël left a reeking city, a pall of smoke lying over it from the bonfires, the stench of death in the air.

'What will become of them?' Celie said in a whisper as they passed through the city gates. 'What is happening to us?'

'I don't know,' Madame replied, her face ashen. 'It seems that an abyss opens up behind each man who acquires authority, and as soon as he steps backwards he falls into it. It can only get worse! I shudder for all those good and decent people we leave behind.' She leaned across a little, her eyes shadowed by concern. 'My dear, did you manage to warn your friend?'

'Yes!' Celie answered with a sweet rush of gratitude. It was the only precious thing left in this descent into hell. 'Yes . . . I warned him. And he will get Amandine out of the city too. I know he cares for her very much.' Why should it hurt her to say that? It was foolish, a childish pain of loneliness, a yearning for what she could not have.

'Amandine?' Madame said with surprise. 'Oh, I am glad. I always liked her. It was good of you to care, my dear, after what happened. Who does she know that was wanted by the Revolution?'

'Georges Coigny . . . her lover.' Again the words hurt.

'Oh!' Madame tried to laugh, but her throat was dry and it was only a curve of the lips and a little cough. 'He is not her lover—he is her cousin, although they were raised together and are more like brother and sister. He is very handsome, don't you think? Thérèse was in love with him, only she is a very selfish woman, I'm afraid, and he threw her over, not very gently, and she has never forgiven him for it. She holds a grudge, does Thérèse. Not a nice quality. Life is too tragically, desperately short, my dear. One should forgive, for one's own sake as much as anything . . . don't you think?'

Celie leaned back in the seat, tears of relief spilling down her cheeks. She was smiling, filled with an uprushing warmth inside that spread through her whole body.

'Yes . . . yes, I do,' she said passionately.